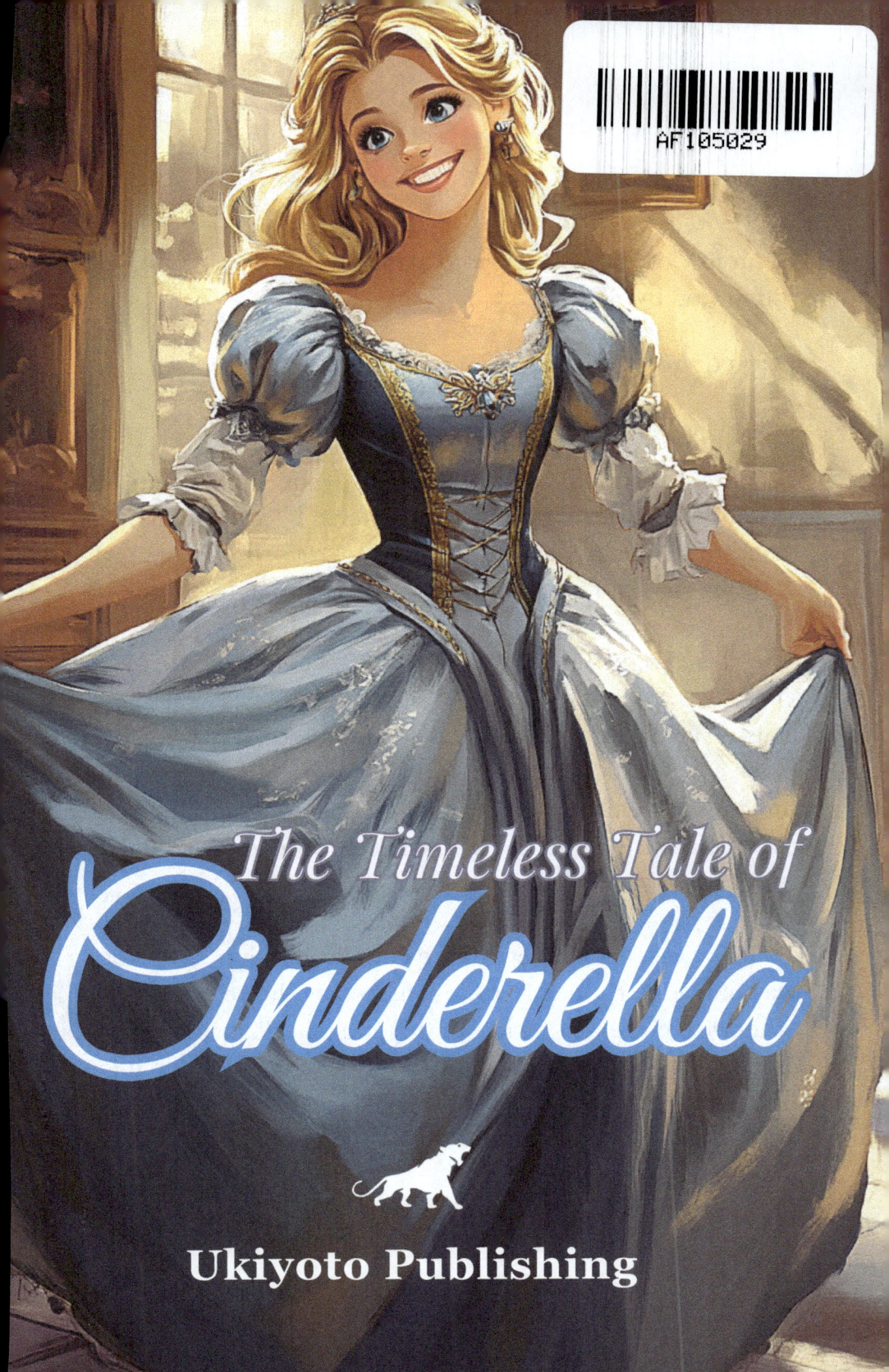

Ukiyoto Publishing

Published in 2025

Content Copyright © Ukiyoto Publishing
Illustrated by SRAC

ISBN 9789370098398

All rights reserved.
No part of this publication may be reproduced, transmitted, or stored in a retrieval system, in any form by any means, electronic, mechanical, photocopying, recording or otherwise, without the prior permission of the publisher.

The moral rights of the authors have been asserted.

This is a work of fiction. Names, characters, businesses, places, events, locales, and incidents are either the products of the author's imagination or used in a fictitious manner. Any resemblance to actual persons, living or dead, or actual events is purely coincidental.

This book is sold subject to the condition that it shall not by way of trade or otherwise, be lent, resold, hired out or otherwise circulated, without the publisher's prior consent, in any form of binding or cover other than that in which it is published.

www.ukiyoto.com

CONTENTS

Chapter One   3

Chapter Two   7

Chapter Three   21

Chapter Four   33

Chapter Five   41

Chapter One

There was once a rich man whose wife lay sick, and when she felt her end drawing near, she called to her only daughter to come near her bed, and said,
"Dear child, be pious and good, and God will always take care of you, and I will look down upon you from heaven and be with you."
And then she closed her eyes and expired. The maiden went every day to her mother's grave, wept, and was always pious and good. When the winter came the snow covered the grave with a white covering, and when the sun came in the early spring and melted it away, the man took to himself another wife.
The new wife brought two daughters. home with her, and they were beautiful and fair in appearance, but at heart were black and ugly. And then began very evil times for the poor stepdaughter.

"Is the stupid creature to sit in the same room with us?" said they; "those who eat food must earn it. Out upon her for a kitchen maid!"

They took away her pretty dresses, put on her an old grey kirtle, and gave her wooden shoes to wear.

"Just look now at the proud princess, how she is decked out!" cried they laughing, and then they sent her into the kitchen. There she was obliged to do heavy work from morning to night, get up early in the morning, draw water, make the fires, cook, and wash. Besides that, the sisters did their utmost to torment her, — mocking her, strewing peas and lentils among the ashes, and setting her to pick them up. In the evenings, when she was quite tired out with her hard day's work, she had no bed to lie on but was obliged to rest on the hearth among the cinders. And as she always looked dusty and dirty, they named her Cinderella.

Chapter Two

It happened one day when the father went to the fair, and he asked his two stepdaughters what he should bring back for them.

"Fine clothes!" said one.

"Pearls and jewels!" said the other.

"But what will you have, Cinderella?" said he.

"The first twig, father, that strikes against your hat on the way home; that is what I should like you to bring me."

So, he bought for the two stepdaughters fine clothes, pearls, and jewels, and on his way back, as he rode through a green lane, a hazel twig struck against his hat; and he broke it off and carried it home with him. And when he reached home, he gave to the step-daughters what they had wished for,

and to Cinderella, he gave the hazel twig. She thanked him, went to her mother's grave, and planted this twig there, weeping so bitterly that the tears fell upon it and watered it, and it flourished and became a fine tree. Cinderella went to see it three times a day and wept and prayed, and each time a white bird rose from the tree, and if she uttered any wish the bird brought her whatever she had wished for.

Now it came to pass that the king ordained a festival that should last for three days, and to which all the beautiful young women of that country were bidden so that the king's son might choose a bride from among them.

When the two step-daughters heard that they too were bidden to appear, they felt very pleased, and they called Cinderella, and said, "Comb our hair, brush our shoes, and make our buckles fast, we are going to the wedding feast at the king's castle."

Cinderella, when she heard this, could not help crying, for she too would have liked to go to the dance, and she begged her stepmother to allow her.

"What, you Cinderella!" said she, "in all your dust and dirt, you want to go to the festival! You have no dress and no shoes! You want to dance!"

But as she persisted in asking, at last, the stepmother said,

"I have strewed a dish full of lentils in the ashes, and if you can pick them all up again in two hours you may go with us."

Then the maiden went to the back door that led into the garden, and called out,

> "O gentle doves, O turtle doves,
> And all the birds that be,
> The lentils that in ashes lie
> Come and pick it up for me!
> The good must be put in the dish,
> The bad you may eat if you wish."

Then there came to the kitchen window two white doves, and after them some turtle doves, and at last a crowd of all the birds under heaven, chirping and fluttering, and they alighted among the ashes; and the doves nodded with their heads and began to pick, peck, pick, peck, and then all the others began to pick, peck, pick, peck, and put all the good grains into the dish.

Before an hour was over all was done, and they flew away. Then the maiden brought the dish to her step-mother, feeling joyful, and thinking that now she should go to the feast; but the step-mother said,

"No, Cinderella, you have no proper clothes, and you do not know how to dance, and you would be laughed at!"

And when Cinderella cried in disappointment, she added,

"If you can pick two dishes full of lentils out of the ashes, nice and clean, you shall go with us," thinking to herself, "for that is not possible." When she had strewed two dishes full of lentils among the ashes the maiden went through the back door into the garden, and cried,

"O gentle doves, O turtle doves,
And all the birds that be,
The lentils that in ashes lie
Come and pick it up for me!
The good must be put in the dish,
The bad you may eat if you wish."

So there came to the kitchen window two white doves, and then some turtle doves, and at last a crowd of all the other birds under heaven, chirping and fluttering, and they alighted among the ashes, and the doves nodded with their heads and began to pick, peck, pick, peck, and then all the others began to pick, peck, pick, peck, and put all the good grains into the dish. And before half an hour was over it was all done, and they flew away.

Then the maiden took the dishes to the step-mother, feeling joyful, and thinking that now she should go with them to the feast; but she said "All this is of no good to you; you cannot come with us, for you have no proper clothes, and cannot dance; you would put us to shame."

Then she turned her back on poor Cinderella and made haste to set out with her two proud daughters.

And as there was no one left in the house, Cinderella went to her mother's grave, under the hazel bush, and cried,

> "Little tree, little tree, shake over me,
> That silver and gold may come down
> and cover me."

Chapter Three

Then the bird threw down a dress of gold and silver, and a pair of slippers embroidered with silk and silver. And in all haste, she put on the dress and went to the festival. But her stepmother and sisters did not know her, and thought she must be a foreign princess, she looked so beautiful in her golden dress. Of Cinderella, they never thought at all, and supposed that she was sitting at home, and picking the lentils out of the ashes. The King's son came to meet her and took her by the hand and danced with her, and he refused to stand up with anyone else so that he might not be obliged to let go of her hand, and when anyone came to claim it, he answered,

"She is my partner."

And when the evening came, she wanted to go home, but the prince said he would go with her to take care of her, for he wanted to see where the beautiful maiden lived. But she escaped him and jumped up into the pigeon house. Then the prince waited until the father came, and told him the strange maiden had jumped into the pigeon-house. The father thought to himself,

"It cannot surely be Cinderella," and called for axes and hatchets, and had the pigeon-house cut down, but there was no one in it. And when they entered the house there sat Cinderella in her dirty clothes among the cinders, and a little oil lamp burnt dimly in the chimney; for Cinderella had been very quick,

and had jumped out of the pigeon house again, and had run to the hazel bush; and there she had taken off her beautiful dress and had laid it on the grave, and the bird had carried it away again, and then she had put on her little grey kirtle again, and had sat down in the kitchen among the cinders.

The next day, when the festival began anew, and the parents and step-sisters had gone to it, Cinderella went to the hazel bush and cried,

> "Little tree, little tree, shake over me,
> That silver and gold may come down
> and cover me."

Then the bird cast down a still more splendid dress than on the day before. And when she appeared in it among the guests one was astonished at her beauty.

The prince had been waiting until she came, and he took her hand and danced with her alone. And when anyone else came to invite her, he said,

"She is my partner."

And when the evening came, she wanted to go home, and the prince followed her, for he wanted to see to what house she belonged; but she broke away from him, and ran into the garden at the back of the house. There stood a fine large tree, bearing splendid pears; she leapt as lightly as a squirrel among the branches, and the prince did not know what had become of her. So, he waited until the father came, and then he told him that the strange maiden had rushed from him and that he thought she had gone up into the pear tree.

The father thought to himself, "It cannot surely be Cinderella," and called for an axe, and felled the tree, but there was no one in it. And when they went into the kitchen there sat Cinderella among the cinders, as usual, for she had got down the other side of the tree, had taken back her beautiful clothes to the bird on the hazel bush, and had put on her old grey kirtle again.

On the third day, when the parents and the step-children had set off, Cinderella went again to her mother's grave, and said to the tree,

"Little tree, little tree, shake over me,
That silver and gold may come down
and cover me."

Then the bird cast down a dress, the like of which had never been seen for splendour and brilliance,

and slippers that were of gold.

And when she appeared in this dress at the feast nobody knew what to say for wonderment. The prince danced with her alone, and if anyone else asked her he answered,

"She is my partner."

And when it was evening Cinderella wanted to go home, and the prince was about to go with her, when she ran past him so quickly that he could not follow her. But he had laid a plan and had caused all the steps to be spread with pitch, so that as she rushed down them the left shoe of the maiden remained sticking in it. The prince picked it up and saw that it was of gold, and very small and slender.

Chapter Four

The next morning, he went to the father and told him that none should be his bride save the one whose foot the golden shoe should fit. Then the two sisters were very glad because they had pretty feet. The eldest went to her room to try on the shoe, and her mother stood by. But she could not get her great toe into it, for the shoe was too small; then her mother handed her a knife, and said,

"Cut the toe off, for when you are queen you will never have to go on foot." So, the girl cut her toe off, squeezed her foot into the shoe, concealed the pain,

and went down to the prince. Then he took her with him on his horse as his bride and rode off. They had to pass by the grave, and there sat the two pigeons on the hazel bush, and cried,

"There they go, there they go!
There is blood on her shoe;
The shoe is too small,
—Not the right bride at all!"

Then the prince looked at her shoe and saw the blood flowing. And he turned his horse round and took the false bride home again, saying she was not the right one, and that the other sister must try on the shoe. So, she went into her room to do so and got her toes comfortably in,

but her heel was too large. Then her mother handed her the knife, saying, "Cut a piece off your heel; when you are queen you will never have to go on foot."

So, the girl cut a piece off her heel and thrust her foot into the shoe, concealed the pain, and went down to the prince, who took his bride before him on his horse and rode off. When they passed by the hazel bush the two pigeons sat there and cried,

"There they go, there they go!
There is blood on her shoe;
The shoe is too small,
—Not the right bride at all!"

Then the prince looked at her foot

and saw how the blood was flowing from the shoe, and staining the white stocking. And he turned his horse round and brought the false bride home again.

"This is not the right one," said he, "have you no other daughter?"

"No," said the man, "only my dead wife left behind her a little stunted Cinderella; it is impossible that she can be the bride." But the King's son ordered her to be sent for, but the mother said,

"Oh no! She is much too dirty; I could not let her be seen."

But he would have her fetched, and so Cinderella had to appear.

Chapter Five

First, she washed her face and hands quite clean and went in and curtseyed to the prince, who held out to her the golden shoe. Then she sat down on a stool, drew her foot out of the heavy wooden shoe, and slipped it into the golden one, which fitted it perfectly. And when she stood up, and the prince looked in her face, he knew again the beautiful maiden that had danced with him, and he cried,
"This is the right bride!"
The stepmother and the two sisters were thunderstruck and grew pale with anger, but he put Cinderella before him on his horse and rode off. As they passed the hazel bush, the two white pigeons cried,

And when they had thus cried, they came flying after and perched on Cinderella's shoulders, one on the right, the other on the left, and so remained.

And when her wedding with the prince was appointed to be held the false sisters came, hoping to curry favour and to take part in the festivities. So as the bridal procession went to the church, the eldest walked on the right side and the younger on the left, and the pigeons picked out an eye of each of them. And as they returned the elder was on the left side and the younger on the right, and the pigeons picked out the other eye of each of them. And so, they were condemned to go blind for the rest of their days because of their wickedness and falsehood.

"Even in the quietest corners, dreams whisper to those who believe."

www.ingramcontent.com/pod-product-compliance
Lightning Source LLC
LaVergne TN
LVHW020416070526
838199LV00054B/3633